Miss Penny had just finished telling them again that they were the *worst* class in the first year.

'For homework,' she barked, 'finish off exercise five if you haven't done so, and do exercise six. Any questions?'

Billy's hand slowly went up.

'Yes, Budge?'

'Please, Miss . . .' Billy hesitated.

'Yes, Budge, what is it?'

'Please, Miss, what's the hardest sum in the world?'

A hush fell over the classroom and all eyes turned on Billy. Miss Penny stared at him. 'What?'

Billy repeated his question.

But, to Billy's astonishment and the delight of his classmates, Miss Penny doesn't know the answer to his question. Promising them an answer tomorrow, she calls in a specialist maths adviser to help. But does *he* know the answer? And, if he doesn't, who does?

D1461223

The Hardest Sum in the World

The Hardest Sum in the World

Terry Wardle
Illustrated by Terry McKenna

CORGI BOOKS

THE HARDEST SUM IN THE WORLD
A CORGI BOOK 0 552 52460 3

Originally published in Great Britain in 1986 by
Andersen Press Limited

PRINTING HISTORY
Corgi edition published 1987
Corgi edition reprinted 1987

This book is set in 12/14 pt Century Schoolbook
by Colset Private Limited, Singapore.

Corgi Books are published by Transworld Publishers
Ltd., 61–63 Uxbridge Road, Ealing, London W5 5SA, in
Australia by Transworld Publishers (Aust.) Pty. Ltd.,
15–23 Helles Avenue, Moorebank, NSW 2170, and in New
Zealand by Transworld Publishers (N.Z.) Ltd., Cnr. Moselle
and Waipareira Avenues, Henderson, Auckland.

Printed and bound in Great Britain by
Cox & Wyman Ltd., Reading, Berks.

The Hardest Sum in the World

Contents

1
Monday Morning

Monday morning! No, it couldn't be. Not so soon. It seemed like hardly any time at all since last Monday.

But it was Monday morning again and Billy Budge peeped cautiously over the bedclothes at it.

Yes, it was definitely a Monday. It had that special dull, grey Monday-morning-ness that was like no other day of the week. It seemed to be glowering in through the curtains at Billy with a face like a cranky old man saying in a deep voice: 'Here I am, Mr Monday Morning. Why are you lying there, Billy, when I'm around?'

'Billy! Get up!' It was his mum's shrill voice from downstairs. 'You'll be late.'

Billy thought about it. He was still thinking about it when, what seemed like

11

moments later, the voice came again, shriller than ever.

'BILL-Y! Are you up? I called you ten minutes ago. Your breakfast is going cold and I am going to be late myself. GET UP!'

It was no good trying to resist Monday morning any longer and Billy crawled out of bed with the feeling that something terrible was going to happen to him.

'It would be much better if I'd stayed in bed,' he muttered to himself as he shuffled to the bathroom.

Fifteen minutes later, downstairs in the kitchen, Billy, now dressed and almost washed, realized what it was that was going to happen to him.

He stopped dead halfway through biting into a piece of toast and a look of horror spread across his chubby face.

'Crumbs,' he gasped, accidentally spitting out bits of marmalady toast, and made a lunge for the corner of the kitchen.

He rummaged behind the fridge, throwing aside his football, the cardboard box from Saturday's shopping, his mum's sandals and his dad's wellingtons and gardening gloves, and snatched up his satchel.

Undoing the straps with trembling fingers he pulled out an exercise book and threw it open. There inside, pointing at him like an accusing finger, was the blank page where Miss Penny's maths homework should have been.

Billy slumped back against the fridge feeling weak and dizzy. Miss Penny would be *furious* when she saw his book. If only he could get out of going to school he could do the homework and hand it in the

13

next day. The more he thought about it, the more he was sure that he wasn't at all well. He had probably got, oh measles, or flu, or plague, or something like that. He wouldn't need to go to school after all.

'Mum,' he called upstairs to the bathroom, 'I can't go to school today, I'm ill.'

A muffled but firm reply came floating down the stairs: 'Rubbish!'

There was only one thing left to do. Billy cleared a space on the table and set to work. He poised his pencil over the blank page, carefully studied the first sum and scratched his head.

When his mum clattered down the stairs from the bathroom in her high heels, wafting perfume into the room, Billy was still scratching his head over the first sum and that dreadful blank page was still staring at him, daring him to scratch some figures on it in his scrawly handwriting.

'What on earth are you doing, Billy?' said his mum. 'Do you know what time it is? Do you ever intend to get to school today?'

'I've got to do this,' he said pleadingly.

14

'Not now. School!'

Billy scratched his head again.

'Why are sums so hard, Mum?'

'They aren't if you can do them,' said his mum.

'Some are,' said Billy.

'Some are harder than others,' said Mum.

2
Miss Penny

Billy Budge was an ordinary sort of boy. At least, there was nothing very extraordinary about him. He lived in a tall, old house, not far from the High Street with his mum and dad, and his gran. His sister, Helen, had lived with them too until she got married the previous September and moved away from the area.

They all called him the baby of the family and his gran, who had been away for what seemed like months visiting Billy's Aunt May, called him 'my little man' and ruffled his hair, which annoyed him, but she also bought him sweets and crisps and smuggled them into his bedroom after he was supposed to have cleaned his teeth and been asleep.

'You have those and don't you say anything to your mum,' she would say to him, as if it was a big secret just between the two of them.

Billy was thinking of his gran as he trudged to school. I wish she would come home again, he thought.

He was a little small for his age, with a face that was a little too chubby and always too grubby. His pockets were always full of bits of string and odds and ends he had picked up and his socks never stayed up, not even when his mum sewed elastic on the tops.

Billy's face grew longer and longer as he trudged on and his socks had fallen as low as they could go without disappearing inside his shoes. He knew when he rounded the next corner he would see school and his heart sank. He liked to see his friends at school and play at break-times and sometimes he thought how nice it would be if they could just do away with the lessons and have one long break-time with dinner in the middle. But until they did Billy would go on hating school, and maths lessons most of all.

'Come on, Billy,' said a voice from behind him. 'You'll be late!' It was his friend 'Jumbo' Gibbs, a small, fat, bespec-

tacled boy who was Billy's best friend at school. Jumbo had been given his rather cruel nickname because of his weight and not because he actually looked anything like an elephant. In fact he was quite good looking, with even features and very blue eyes, but his whole face was now flushed a bright red from rushing, and it was all he could do to find the breath to urge Billy to hurry.

'Don't care,' muttered Billy, trudging slowly on.

'You will if you're late for Miss Penny's class,' said Jumbo.

The mention of Miss Penny made Billy quicken his step slightly. He looked up and saw the school in the distance, a long, low red-brick building squatting beyond open gates at the end of the road like a huge monster with its mouth open ready to swallow children. 'Ugggh,' Billy thought, and he shuddered.

'How long have we got?' he asked Jumbo apprehensively.

Jumbo stared hard at his wrist. 'Don't know,' he said. 'I can't see my watch. My glasses are all steamed up.'

He took out his handkerchief ready to wipe them when, with a sharp shrill squeal like the horrible headless ghost that Billy's gran said she had once seen, the school bell rang out.

'Oh no,' they both cried and began running for the school gates, to be swallowed up in the enormous mass of school uniforms pushing, shoving, shouting and chattering along the corridors to their classrooms.

Miss Penny's room was down a long grey corridor near the science rooms where strange unpleasant smells wafted out of the doors. Perhaps, thought Billy, as he hurried down the corridor, that was why a smell like damp raincoats always seemed to hang around the maths room. He hesitated as he reached the door and tried to think of some reason for not going in.

'Come on, Billy,' said Jumbo from behind. 'She'll be furious if we're not there before her.'

Billy turned the doorhandle and with Jumbo pushing from behind he almost fell into the room. He looked quickly towards the big desk in the corner and breathed a huge sigh of relief when he saw that Miss Penny wasn't there. He looked around and saw the rest of his first year group in their places turning to stare at him and Jumbo. He hurried quickly to his place at the back of the room with Jumbo puffing along behind and sat down heavily.

He wasn't exactly pleased to be there

but he was very pleased that he had arrived before Miss Penny. She liked to make her entrance when the class was sitting ready, books out and politely quiet. She did not like children who arrived late and interrupted her lesson.

Billy slumped down in his seat and looked around at the rest of the class. They were one of four first year groups at Dashwood High School, but they had almost completed the year and were looking forward to going into the second year after the summer holidays, when they would no longer be the babies of the school.

Most of the children came from the big council estate behind the school, others from the big private houses in front of the school and a few, like Billy, from further away.

Billy's class had already got a reputation for being the worst one in the first year, thanks to 'Croaker' Harris and his pals, who fooled around in every lesson, except Miss Penny's. Croaker had probably earned his nickname because of his hoarse voice but his pals picked it up from his mum, who never seemed to call him by his real name, Steven. Everyone called him Croaker behind his back, but anyone who wasn't a pal of his who called him that would probably get a punch on the nose.

As Billy looked around he saw that several of the children were hurriedly comparing answers to their homework sums and busily correcting them. He realized that he could be taking this chance to get his homework done. He quickly got out his books and took up where he had left off at the breakfast table, scratching his head over the first sum. But he didn't go unnoticed for long. Croaker Harris, who was sitting nearby, leaned over to take a closer look, then said: 'What you doin', Budge?'

'Nothing,' said Billy defensively.

'Nothing?' repeated Croaker hoarsely. 'Let's 'ave a look.' He reached out and grabbed the book before Billy could stop him. Croaker peered at the page, blank except for the heading, 'Homework', then he held the book up and shouted hoarsely: 'Hey look, Billy Budge hasn't done 'is homework.'

He turned to Billy with a nasty grin on

his face. 'I'm going to show this to Miss and she'll murder you,' he said. The thought pleased him, and he shouted to the class: 'Hey, Miss is going to murder him.'

Billy jumped up and was trying to grab the book back when the classroom door opened. Into the room walked the dreaded Miss Penny, peering at the class through her thick horn-rimmed spectacles like the science teacher peering at specimens through a microscope.

Billy sat down as if he had been pulled back by a spring. Croaker threw the exercise book back onto Billy's desk and gave him another malicious grin.

Miss Penny stared round at the class, waiting impatiently for everyone to settle.

'Good morning, 14b,' she said.

'Good morning, Miss Penny,' the class chanted obediently.

A dreadful silence fell over the class as Miss Penny stared around. Pupils squirmed in their seats as her gaze fell on them.

'I cannot see many books open,' said Miss Penny icily. 'Just because I am held up for a few minutes it does not follow that the class has to start late. You all know what time we are due to start and you can all see the clock. I assume you can all tell the time?' She gazed round the classroom again, creating squirms wherever she looked. 'Well, let's not waste any more time, 14b. Open your textbooks at page twenty-two and continue with the next exercise straight away.'

Amid the frantic rustling of pages a hand shot up and someone asked: 'Please, Miss, is that exercise four?'

'No,' said Miss Penny icily. 'You have already done exercise four for homework.' She gave the class another squirm-making stare. 'I hope you *have* all done the homework.' Billy winced.

Miss Penny sat down at her desk in the corner and opened her register while the class silently bent their heads over their books to struggle with exercise five.

'Andrews,' barked Miss Penny.

'Yes, Miss?' said the startled pupil.

'Bring your homework.'

Billy's heart sank down to the deepest depths of his tummy, for his name came next. He listened apprehensively as the luckless Andrews was told off for getting two sums wrong and not knowing how to do another one.

'All right,' barked Miss Penny, 'back to your place.' Billy broke out into a cold sweat. 'Budge,' she called out. 'Bring your book.'

Billy obediently picked up the exercise book with the blank homework page and stumbled out to Miss Penny's desk, his feet feeling like great lead weights. Croaker Harris gave him a nasty grin as Billy passed his desk.

'Give me your book,' said Miss Penny, holding out her hand.

'Please, Miss. . .'

'Just a minute,' said Miss Penny impatiently. 'Let me see your homework first.'

'But, Miss. . .'

'Give me your book,' snapped Miss Penny angrily.

There was nothing for it but to hand over the book. Miss Penny stared at the blank page and then at the pages either side of it. 'Where is your homework, Budge?'

'Please, Miss, that's what I was trying to tell you, Miss, I couldn't . . . do it.'

Billy heard his voice gradually dying away. There were gasps of horror from his classmates.

'You haven't done it?' Miss Penny stared at him in astonishment. 'You haven't done it?'

'Please, Miss, I couldn't do it,' Billy pleaded.

Miss Penny began to recover from the shock. 'Why not? Everyone else managed to do it.' She got up and strode angrily towards the class. 'Is there anyone else who hasn't done it?' she asked, daring anyone to put up a hand. 'There you are,' she said triumphantly, turning to Billy. 'Everyone else has managed to do the homework, Budge. So why couldn't you?'

Billy muttered: 'Don't know, Miss.'

'Don't know? Don't know? I'll see you after the lesson, Budge. Sit down.'

Billy's face turned bright red as he returned to his desk past the grinning Croaker Harris and his cronies.

Miss Penny was in an especially bad mood for the rest of the lesson, telling off anyone who had got even one of their homework sums wrong, and quite a few unpleasant looks were thrown in Billy's direction by his classmates as they returned, red-faced, from Miss Penny's desk.

Billy sank deeper down behind his desk and scratched his head over exercise five, which was even worse than exercise four. With just ten minutes of the lesson to go Billy had only got two answers and he wasn't sure those were right.

'You should all have finished exercise five by now,' Miss Penny called out.

Billy looked again at the two answers on his page and scratched his head. Why were sums so hard, he thought.

Miss Penny was telling them all how much harder the work was going to be when they got into the second year and how some of them — Billy fancied she was glaring in his direction — would have to pull their socks up considerably if they thought there was anything hard about the work they were doing now.

Billy groaned inwardly. He closed his eyes and had a sudden vision of pages and pages of sums that he couldn't do stretching into the future. The figures got bigger and bigger until they seemed to tower over him, clustered round his desk like dozens of impatient, glaring Miss Pennys. How much worse could it get, he wondered. At least it might not seem so bad if he knew the worst possible sum he might ever have to do. Perhaps if he knew the answer to that all the other easier sums might not seem so bad.

Miss Penny had just finished telling them again that they were the *worst* class in the first year.

'For homework,' she barked, 'finish off

exercise five if you haven't done so, and do exercise six. Any questions?'

Billy's hand slowly went up.

'Yes, Budge?'

'Please, Miss. . .' Billy hesitated.

'Yes, Budge, what is it?'

'Please, Miss, what's the hardest sum in the world?'

A hush fell over the classroom and all eyes turned on Billy. Miss Penny stared at him. 'What?'

Billy repeated his question. Miss Penny blinked at him from behind her heavy spectacles. She had liked doing sums ever since she was at school and had done hundreds, thousands, perhaps even millions of them. But she had never thought about which was the hardest one she had done, let alone which was the hardest in the world. Miss Penny blushed bright red as she realized that Billy Budge had asked her a question she couldn't answer. She looked at Billy and at the class waiting expectantly for an answer and she began to feel very hot and flustered.

'Well,' she began slowly, 'some sums are harder than others, of course. . .'

The class began to stir into life, realiz-

ing that the dreaded Miss Penny was on the defensive.

'Yes, Miss, but what *is* the hardest one?' called out Croaker Harris, sensing a chance to have some fun at the expense of the teacher.

'Well, I think the hardest sum is. . .' Miss Penny was now as red as a beetroot and sweat broke out on her forehead. 'Well. . .'

Outside in the corridor the bell suddenly rang signalling the end of the lesson. Miss Penny breathed a huge sigh of relief.

'Off you go now,' she called out. 'Off to break.'

Some of the children got up but quickly sat down again when they received menacing glances from Croaker and his pals. The children sat waiting patiently.

'Well, off you go,' said Miss Penny impatiently.

The class stirred slightly but no one got up.

Croaker's hand shot up. 'Please, Miss, you didn't answer the question.' He was grinning his nasty grin.

'Oh, there's no time for that now. You'll be late for break.'

Billy began to feel quite sorry for Miss Penny and wished he hadn't asked the question. He put up his hand. 'Please, Miss. . .'

'Not now, Billy.'

'But, Miss. . .'

'Please, Miss, I thought perhaps you could answer the question tomorrow.'

'Yes,' said Miss Penny brightly, 'yes, that's it. I'll answer your question tomorrow. Now off you go, 14b, quietly off to break.'

And with that Miss Penny rushed out, quite forgetting that she was going to see Billy about his homework.

She rushed downstairs into the staff-room where the other teachers were already drinking their morning tea and complaining about their classes, and slumped into a chair.

'What is it, dear?' asked Miss Brogan, the RE teacher. 'You look as if you've had a nasty shock.'

'Not at all,' said Miss Penny icily. But it had been a shock to be stumped by Billy Budge of all people. He was one of the most hopeless children in all her first year maths classes. What on earth could have made him ask that question? And how could she possibly find the answer by tomorrow? Miss Penny shuddered at the thought of facing 14b again without the answer. She urgently needed help and advice and it suddenly occurred to her where she could get it. She quickly grabbed the staffroom telephone.

'Hello,' she said, 'is Mr Fletcher there, please? Yes, it is urgent. Hello, Mr Fletcher? I know you must be busy. . . Yes, this is Miss Penny . . . Mr Fletcher, I wondered if . . . Yes, I am fine, thank you . . . Mr Fletcher, I wondered if you could come along to see me at school tomorrow morning. Yes, I know you must be busy. Yes, it is very urgent. Yes, but I would be most grateful if . . . You will? Oh, that's marvellous. Yes, tomorrow morning, about 9 o'clock. Yes, thank you, that's very kind of you.'

3

Mr Fletcher and the Computer

There was a sense of excitement in the air when the maths class assembled the next morning. When Billy arrived, late as usual, he found a very different attitude to him. Instead of the usual indifferent stares he was greeted warmly and patted on the back like a hero.

As he slipped into his place at the back of the class, Croaker Harris turned and grinned at him with a new respect. 'You caught her out there, didn't you, Billy?' grinned Croaker.

'Yeah,' said Croaker's cronies. 'Ask her again, Billy. She promised to answer you today. Make sure she does. Ask her again, Billy.'

All this sudden popularity took Billy completely by surprise. He had never been the most popular boy in the class and was usually just happy if the others ignored him, especially Croaker and his pals. It was very nice suddenly to be the centre of attention but it also worried Billy. He seemed to have hit on a streak of dislike, almost hatred, of Miss Penny among the other children which he didn't share. He dreaded Miss Penny's lessons and he didn't like her very much but he hadn't asked his question to cause her trouble and he didn't want to make her upset and flustered again as she had been the previous day. He was afraid the other children would be very disappointed if they knew how he really felt and every time they grinned and patted him on the back he felt like a fraud.

He hadn't thought much more about his question. For the rest of the previous day his class had been split up into groups for French, woodwork and home economics and Billy hadn't seen most of them since the previous morning. During the evening he had stumbled painfully through the two maths exercises left for homework and with the help of his dad he managed to come up with answers of sorts to all the sums.

When he had thought of the question he had felt rather sorry for having asked it, remembering how embarrassed Miss Penny had been. But his classmates saw a chance to turn the tables on the dreaded maths teacher who had so often made them tremble and they were not about to throw it away. They chattered excitedly as they waited for Miss Penny to arrive but as the minutes ticked by there was still no sign of her.

'Maybe she ain't coming,' said Croaker hoarsely. 'Maybe she's scared of Billy.'

Then suddenly a cry went up from someone near the window: 'There she is!'

There was a scramble for the window and twenty-eight pairs of eyes stared down at the staff car park. Miss Penny was hurrying out from the front entrance to greet a tall burly man who was getting out of his car. The children began asking each other who he was but no one had ever seen him before. They wondered what his appearance could mean.

The man had a short conversation with Miss Penny, then they hurried towards the front entrance and disappeared inside. The members of class 14b went on staring at the empty car park as if they were hypnotised, until someone shouted: 'Come on quickly, she'll be here in a minute.'

They shot back to their places and sat waiting expectantly but there was no longer the same sense of excitement in the air. Everyone wondered who the burly man was and why he was there. What could it mean? They began to fear that Billy's question might mean trouble for all of them.

Moments later Miss Penny and the burly man hurried into the room. He looked even bigger close up and towered over Miss Penny as he stood beside her at the front of the class.

'Good morning, 14b,' Miss Penny trilled.

'Good morning, Miss Penny,' they muttered obediently.

'Today children we are privileged to have with us Mr Fletcher,' said Miss Penny. 'He is the maths adviser to all the schools in the area so he is a very busy man but he has kindly agreed to come here today and see us. Isn't that good of him, children?'

'Yes, Miss,' they muttered.

Mr Fletcher gave a sort of half smile like a huge snake opening its mouth to eat you up. 'Don't you worry about me, children,' he said. 'I'll just tuck myself away somewhere and you won't even know I'm here.'

He seated himself at a desk in the corner, towering at least two feet above the children sitting around him, then he took some papers out of his brief-case and began rustling them noisily and humming to himself. The children watched his every move apprehensively.

Miss Penny clapped her hands to get attention. 'Open your books and get on with the next exercise,' she commanded.

The class went on as normal, except that Mr Fletcher hummed and rustled in the corner and Miss Penny didn't call the children out to mark their homework, much to Billy's annoyance since he had managed to do it.

But behind the near silence the class seethed with tension. Billy's unanswered question was on the minds of all his classmates, even though, to tell the truth, none of them had thought about what the

answer might be or even why it might be
worth trying to find out.

The other children kept darting glances
at Billy and he knew they were waiting for
him to ask his question again. Finally he
couldn't put it off any longer.

Miss Penny saw Billy's hand go up and
leapt to her feet as if she had been shot
from a gun. Mr Fletcher stopped hum-

ming and rustling and a hush fell on the room.

'Yes, Billy?' Miss Penny said.

'Please, Miss, you said you would answer my question today.'

'Which question was that, Billy?' asked Miss Penny coldly, as if daring him to repeat it.

'Please, Miss, what is the hardest sum in the world?'

The children were startled by a loud creaking noise from the corner of the room as Mr Fletcher rose out of the chair which had been groaning under his weight. All eyes were on him as he sauntered to the front of the class.

'That's a very good question, isn't it, Miss Penny?' He gave another of his dangerous looking half smiles.

'Yes, it is a good question,' said Miss Penny.

'And who is this young man, Miss Penny?'

'This is Billy Budge, Mr Fletcher.'

'Billy Budge, eh.' Mr Fletcher took a step forward and peered at Billy as if he couldn't quite believe his eyes. Billy was turning very red. 'A keen young mathematician, eh, Miss Penny?'

'I wouldn't say that, Mr Fletcher.'

'No,' said Mr Fletcher, frowning. 'No?' He advanced on Billy and stood towering over his desk. Picking up Billy's maths book he leafed through it making odd grunting noises that didn't sound promising, then dropped the book back on the desk as if he feared he might catch something from it.

'Don't you like maths, Billy?'

'No, sir, not very much,' said Billy, turning even redder than before.

'Oh. Mmmm,' murmured Mr Fletcher. Then he snapped: 'What's five nines plus two tens divided by fourteen to the nearest three decimal places?'

'Ahhh. It's . . . um . . . well it's. . .'

'Come along, boy. All right then, here's an easy one, what's the square root of sixteen?'

Billy wondered what on earth a square root was.

'All right, here's a really easy one. What's four divided by four, multiplied by two, doubled?'

'It's . . . um. . .' Billy's mind had gone completely blank. All the figures jumbled

and tumbled around in his head until he couldn't even grasp the question, let alone think of an answer. Mr Fletcher stood back with a satisfied smile.

'Well, well, Billy *isn't* very good at maths, is he, Miss Penny?'

'No, he isn't, Mr Fletcher.'

'Well, young man,' said Mr Fletcher, sauntering back to the front of the class, 'my advice to you is to work hard at the easy sums before you start thinking about the hard ones. There'll be plenty of time for you to worry about those later when you are in the exam class. But,' he added with a smug grin, 'I don't think you, young man, will ever have to worry about what is the hardest one of all. No, no, I don't think you will be going anything like that far.'

He grinned at Billy, satisfied with his handling of the problem, but Billy, who had been blushing with embarrassment, began to go hot with anger. Mr Fletcher had tricked him. Just because he couldn't answer Mr Fletcher's sums it didn't mean he couldn't want to know about the hardest sums. If Mr Fletcher was so clever, why couldn't he answer the question? Miss Penny was trying to dismiss the class when Billy's hand shot up.

'Yes, Billy?'

'Please, Miss, you promised you would answer my question.'

'Mr Fletcher has dealt with your question, Billy,' said Miss Penny coldly.

Billy persisted. 'Please, Miss, he hasn't. He didn't tell me the answer.'

'I have dealt with your question, young man,' said Mr Fletcher sternly.

'No, you 'aven't,' called out a hoarse

voice. 'Answer his question.'

The other children, encouraged by Croaker's interruption, started calling out. 'Yeah, answer his question,' they shouted. 'Tell him what he wants to know.'

'Please, Mr Fletcher,' said Billy, 'if you know the answer to my question, can't you tell me?'

'No, I can't,' snapped Mr Fletcher.

'He don't know it,' shouted Croaker and children around the class took up the shout.

Mr Fletcher was feeling hot and getting very red in the face. He had not had an experience like this since he was a young student teacher. Children did not usually dare to disobey him.

'Silence!' he shouted.

For a moment the children were startled, then the noise of chattering and calling out started again. Mr Fletcher, his red face now turning white, took a step back and trod on Miss Penny's foot.

'Oh, I'm terribly sorry. What are we going to do now?'

'I had hoped you would know that, Mr Fletcher,' said Miss Penny. 'If only we could work out the answer somehow.'

'Yes,' said Mr Fletcher excitedly, 'that's it. Work it out. That's it. Well done, Miss Penny.' He took the startled Miss Penny by the arms and shook her excitedly.

'Well done, well done,' he said. He turned to the class and with some difficulty made himself heard. 'Children, I have the answer.'

There was suddenly complete silence as looks first of surprise and then of disappointment spread across the faces of Billy's classmates who feared their fun was now over.

'What is it then?' called a hoarse voice.

'Yes, well, you see, children, when I say I have it I don't mean I actually have it on me.'

A groan of disbelief spread around the class.

'Wait a minute, wait a minute, what I mean is that I can get it.'

The class waited expectantly and Mr Fletcher adopted what he thought would be a calming tone of voice. 'You see, children, nowadays people don't need to carry all sorts of basic information in their heads. We store information in big machines called computers and when we want it we just go and get it out. And you are in luck because one of the very best computers in the world is at the university not many miles from here and it's run by a friend of mine. I am going that way when I leave here so I'll drop in and see my friend, get the answer to Billy's question, and you'll have it by ... oh ... tomorrow ... perhaps.'

While the children were taking in this information Mr Fletcher and Miss Penny saw their chance and gathering up their things they hurried out of the room. Most of the break had already gone and Miss Penny had to hurry straight off to another lesson.

'Thank you for coming to help,' she told Mr Fletcher, thinking that he hadn't been much help.

'Not at all, and don't worry, Miss Penny, I'll make sure young Billy gets his answer.' By post, he thought as he hurried away. He had not had such an experience with a class for many years and was not keen to repeat it.

But Mr Fletcher's troubles were not

over. When he arrived at the university computer building he found that his friend had a cold and was not at work. He was introduced to the computer technician, a nervous, bearded little man called Mr Wright, who agreed to help.

'What do you want to do with the computer?' asked Mr Wright as they walked down the corridor to the main computer room.

'I want to find the answer to a very complicated maths problem,' replied Mr Fletcher importantly.

They went into a large modern room full of expensive-looking machinery. Mr Wright showed Mr Fletcher a keyboard like a typewriter with a screen like a television set above it.

'If you type out the problem the computer will give you the solution,' said Mr Wright.

Mr Fletcher could not type and it took a lot of searching around for the right letters before his question was printed up on the screen. Mr Wright looked over Mr Fletcher's shoulder and blinked when he read the sentence: 'What is the hardest sum in the world?'

The computer was silent for a moment, then it printed up the answer: 'Go boil your head, ape face!'

Mr Fletcher stared at the screen in disbelief and began to turn purple with anger. It was bad enough to have an awful morning with those terrible kids, but now he had a stupid machine insulting him.

Mr Wright coughed nervously. 'It's

programmed to answer like that if the students ask it . . . um . . . silly questions.'

Mr Fletcher drew himself up to his full height, towering over Mr Wright. 'Are you suggesting that I am asking a silly question?' he asked unpleasantly.

'No, well, I was only saying that . . . well . . . perhaps I can try.' Mr Wright leaned over the machine and pressed several keys, then expertly tapped out the question on the keyboard. They both watched the screen intently. After a few moments the message 'No data' appeared on the screen.

'What does that mean?' demanded Mr Fletcher. Mr Wright didn't answer but tapped out a message asking the computer to give a fuller explanation.

After a few seconds a message appeared. Mr Fletcher started reading aloud: 'No data has been programmed which can allow an answer to this question. A prior requirement of any answer would be further information on the terms involved. For example, what is meant by "hardest"? Hardest for whom? Under what circumstances? In what. . .' Mr Fletcher broke off reading the long message on the screen. 'It doesn't know,' he said angrily. 'Your machine doesn't know the answer, does it?'

Mr Wright seemed to be turning red under his beard. 'Well, it isn't that it doesn't know. It is trying to tell you that there are some problems about the answer.'

'There's only one problem,' said Mr Fletcher angrily. 'It doesn't know the answer.'

Mr Wright, who was very proud of the computer and what it could do, was also getting angry. 'It could answer the question if you asked it correctly,' he said.

'There's nothing wrong with my question,' snapped Mr Fletcher.

'Yes, there is,' snapped Mr Wright. 'It's ... it's ... silly.'

'Silly? Silly?' repeated Mr Fletcher. 'How dare you call me silly!'

Mr Wright, almost speechless with rage, snapped out the first thing that came into his head: 'Oh, go and boil your head, ape face!'

Mr Fletcher snorted with rage and stormed off out of the building. Mr Wright was also in a terrible temper. He went back to his office and sat fuming about how rude Mr Fletcher had been.

'I know what I'll do,' Mr Wright muttered to himself as he reached for the telephone. 'I'll fix him ... Hello —' he said, 'is that the *Daily Chronicle*? Good. I have got some news for you.'

4

The *Chronicle*

The next day an item about Mr Fletcher appeared in the *Daily Chronicle*. It was only a small item but it was read by millions of people all over the country who chuckled at it over their breakfast tables. But when Mr Fletcher's boss read it he did not chuckle. He flew into a rage and swore this would be the end of Mr Fletcher as a maths adviser. *The* end.

Miss Penny read it and most of the children in class 14b had either seen it or heard about it. By the time word had got round of Mr Fletcher's visit to the school the previous day and the reason for it, the school was buzzing with excitement.

One of the few people who had not seen the *Chronicle* was Mr Fletcher himself. He went to his office as usual, quite unaware of all the fuss he had caused, and was surprised to find a message telling him to see his boss straight away.

'Ah, Fletcher,' snarled his boss. 'Sit down.'

Mr Fletcher knew he was in real trouble and began to feel rather like a fly trapped in a spider's web.

'I hear you were out and about yesterday,' his boss continued. 'Paying a visit to the university, were you?'

'Yes, I did drop in there for a few minutes,' said Mr Fletcher, wondering how his boss knew. Perhaps the technician had complained about the row they had.

'The computer department, was it?' snarled his boss.

'Yes, that's right, sir. And if you have heard from the technician there I would just like to say. . .'

'Technician?' interrupted his boss. 'Technician? What are you rambling about?'

'Well, you see, sir, there was some trouble with the technician. . .'

'This is the only trouble you need to worry about,' snapped his boss, hurling the *Daily Chronicle* across the desk. 'Do you know you have turned this department into a laughing stock? I have had half a dozen councillors on the phone to me this morning screaming blue murder about this. I have been pestered by other newspapers, radio stations, television news... I don't mind telling you, Fletcher, that it will be a miracle if you are still working for this department after all the fuss dies down. *A* miracle.'

Mr Fletcher was not really listening. He was staring blankly at the *Chronicle*, reading an item at the top of the page over and over again. It read:

MATHS EXPERT GOES APE

A computer made a monkey of a maths expert yesterday.

James Fletcher, maths adviser to Keyside Education Authority, asked a university computer for information.

But it called him 'ape face' and told him: 'Go boil your head.'

Mr Fletcher angrily complained the machine had gone wrong.

But a staff member said: 'The computer is programmed to give silly answers to silly questions.'

'Well,' snapped the boss, 'what have you got to say for yourself?'

But Mr Fletcher could only stare at the newspaper and shake his head. 'I don't understand,' he said slowly. 'I don't understand. How could they have known?'

'That doesn't matter,' snapped the

boss. 'The point is that you are in real trouble this time, Fletcher. *Real* trouble. You'll hear more of this, believe me.'

At the offices of the *Daily Chronicle* the editor had also been reading the news item. He reached for the phone and called one of his best reporters up to his office.

'This item on page three about the maths expert and the computer,' he said when the reporter arrived. 'I sense a bigger story here. Get over to the university and find out what this fellow was asking the computer.'

'Okay, chief,' said the reporter. In less than an hour he had seen the computer technician at the university and knew what Mr Fletcher's question had been. Why on earth would he want to ask a question like that, wondered the reporter. There was only one way to find out.

Mr Fletcher was sitting in his office, still smarting from the interview with his boss, when the phone rang.

'Mr Fletcher? This is Craig Grant from the *Daily Chronicle*.'

'*Daily Chronicle*?' said Mr Fletcher, trying to collect his thoughts. '*Daily Chronicle*?'

'I wanted to find out why you were asking the computer that particular question at the university yesterday?'

'*Daily Chronicle*!' snorted Mr Fletcher. 'You've got a nerve ringing me up. Do you know you've made my department a laughing stock? Councillors have been screaming blue murder about this. Do you know it will be a miracle if I stay in my job after all this fuss? Do you know. . .'

'Steady on. Steady on,' interrupted the reporter.

'Steady on?' repeated Mr Fletcher. 'Would you steady on if you were in my place?'

'Just keep calm, chief,' said the reporter. 'You never know, we might be able to do something about your problems.'

'What could you do?'

'Never underestimate the power of the press, chief,' said the reporter. 'If we can get you in trouble, we can get you out again.'

'Could you?' said Mr Fletcher, brightening up a bit.

'No problem,' said the reporter. 'Just tell me the whole story.'

So Mr Fletcher told him about Billy's question, Miss Penny's call for help, Billy's class and the problem with the computer.

'Great,' said the reporter. 'Don't you worry, chief. Just leave everything to me. I'll make you a hero by tomorrow.'

'Oh,' said Mr Fletcher doubtfully, not at all sure that he wanted to be a hero.

'No problem,' said the reporter. 'By the way, I'll be sending a photographer along to get a picture of you later. And don't worry, everything is going to be great.'

'Great,' said Mr Fletcher, doubtfully.

The reporter collected a photographer and went straight to Dashwood High School. While he was waiting for Miss Penny to finish a lesson he asked the school secretaries what they knew about Billy and his question. He went out into the corridor and asked children who had been sent out from classes on errands. He even asked the school odd-job man when he passed by with his ladder and tools. By lunchtime the reporter had been told a lot about Billy and the things that had been happening, not all of it exactly right, and some of it totally wrong.

Miss Penny was surprised to find the reporter waiting for her in the corridor and amazed when he said he had been told she was the person responsible for young Billy's great love of mathematics.

'Oh, well, I don't think . . .' stuttered Miss Penny. 'You see, he isn't exactly. . .'

'You shouldn't be so modest,' said the reporter. 'It's a great thing to be able to shape impressionable young minds. I only wish I had your ability.'

'Oh, no,' said Miss Penny, blushing. 'I don't really think I have all that much. . .'

'Nonsense,' said the reporter. 'Where would we be without people like you to guide the youth of the nation? Now, tell me all about this question young Billy has been asking.'

Billy, meanwhile, had no idea of the interest he had aroused. He knew nothing of Mr Fletcher's trouble with his boss or of the trouble the reporter had been going to to trace him and find out about his question. He quite liked all the attention he had been getting, this time not just from members of his class but children in all the other classes and even the teachers. Children he didn't know had been patting him on the back and saying, 'Well done, Billy,' as they passed him in the corridors and even much bigger pupils had been stopping him and asking about how he had got Mr Fletcher to go and try to use the computer. But it also worried him, because he had a nagging suspicion that Mr Fletcher might come back to the school and blame him for all the trouble over the computer.

At lunchtime he tried to get away from the others by hiding in a corner of the playground but he was quickly spotted and pointed out to the reporter who had been looking for him all over the school, much to the annoyance of the headmaster.

'Hello, Billy,' said the young reporter, sitting down beside him. 'Do you know who I am?'

'No, sir,' said Billy politely.

'I'm Craig Grant from the *Daily Chronicle*,' said the reporter with a grin, pushing back a lock of his fair hair that seemed to be forever trying to fall across his face. 'I'll bet you've heard of the *Daily Chronicle*.'

'Yes, sir,' said Billy, very much afraid

Mr Fletcher might have sent the reporter to tell him off about the computer.

'You've been causing your teachers a few problems, I hear,' said the reporter with a grin. 'Why don't you tell me about it?'

'Well . . . I am sorry Mr Fletcher got

into trouble with the computer. I never meant that to happen.'

'Oh, don't worry about that,' said the reporter. 'Tell me all about this question you asked.'

'I just asked Miss Penny what's the hardest sum in the world,' said Billy, wondering why the *Daily Chronicle* should be interested.

'What gave you the idea to ask that?'

'I don't know,' said Billy truthfully. With all the fuss and worry about Mr Fletcher and the computer his mind had gone completely blank. He kept trying to sort out his thoughts and remember what he had really wanted to know when he first asked the question, but the ideas all kept jumbling up in his head and the day before yesterday seemed a very long time ago.

'You've got a real thirst for knowledge, eh?'

'I suppose so,' said Billy doubtfully, not at all sure what a thirst for knowledge was.

'Great,' said the reporter, scribbling in his notebook and already writing the story in his head. Schoolboy stumps his teachers *and* a computer, he thought. Great stuff. Might even make the front page.

Billy's mum was woken early next morning. She gradually realized that the phone was ringing and as she reached out from under the covers to fumble for it on the bedside locker she caught sight of the alarm clock. She rubbed her eyes and looked again. Yes, it was definitely 6.30 a.m.

'Hello,' said a bright voice on the phone, 'Keyside Radio here. About this question your son has been asking. We'd like to get something on our early bulletin at 7 a.m. Can you just give me a few details about him. You know the sort of thing — what he's good at in school, how proud you are of him and so on.'

'What?' Billy's mum blinked and tried to make some sense of what the voice was saying. 'Who is this?' she asked, peering at the clock again.

'I just told you,' said the voice sounding irritated, 'this is Keyside Radio.'

'Do you know what time it is?' demanded Billy's mum.

'It's just 6.32 a.m.,' said the voice

brightly. 'You ought to listen in, you
know. We give time checks every seven
minutes in the morning.'

'I know what time it is,' said Billy's
mum angrily.

'Oh, good,' said the voice, 'now about
this question your son has been asking.'

'What question? What are you talking
about?'

'Your son, Billy Budge. The story in the

Chronicle, "Schoolboy Baffles Brains".'

'What story? About my Billy?'

'You must have seen it,' said the voice, but Billy's mum wasn't listening anymore. She was poking frantically at Billy's sleeping dad.

'Brian, Brian, there's a man on the phone who says there's something about our Billy in the *Chronicle*. Brian, wake up.'

A deep voice from underneath the bedclothes said sleepily: 'Forget it. It's one of those crank calls.'

'No it isn't, Brian. It's the radio station. They say our Billy is in the *Chronicle*,' and with a massive pull she wrenched the bedclothes off Billy's dad. 'Quick, Brian,' she shouted, 'go and get a paper.' Then she shot into Billy's room shouting: 'Come on, Billy, get up. You've done it this time. What have you been up to?'

By the time Billy was awake enough to start trying to explain to his mum about the things that had been happening the phone was ringing again. It rang twice more with calls from newspapers before Billy's dad got back from the paper shop with a copy of the *Chronicle*.

They took the phone off the hook and gathered round the kitchen table with the paper laid out on it, Billy and his mum still in their nightclothes and Billy's dad with some clothes thrown quickly on over his pyjamas.

This time there wasn't just a short item on an inside page but a big story covering most of the front page, with pictures of Mr Fletcher, Miss Penny and Billy himself.

'Billy,' gasped his mum, looking horrified, 'what have you done?'

Billy winced. I knew there would be trouble over this, he thought.

Billy's dad, who had already read the story on his way back from the paper shop, began to read it again out loud. It read:

SCHOOLBOY BAFFLES BRAIN

A SCHOOLBOY has baffled his teacher and a maths expert with a question they couldn't answer.

Even a computer was beaten by Billy

Budge's passion for mathematical knowledge.

What the chubby 11-year-old wanted to know was: 'What is the hardest sum in the world?'

Billy, a first year pupil at Dashwood High School, Keyside, put this question to his maths teacher.

Miss Monica Penny, who teaches first year maths there, called in maths adviser James Fletcher.

Miss Penny said: 'Billy and his classmates were very keen to find the answer.'

Mr Fletcher, adviser for maths to all the schools in Keyside, took the question to the computer at nearby Keyside University.

He told the *Chronicle*: 'The computer just didn't have a clue and neither did the technician if you ask me.'

Billy told our reporter yesterday: 'I don't know why I asked the question. I suppose I just have a thirst for knowledge.'

But despite the dedicated efforts of his teachers, Billy is still waiting for an answer.

Anyone who has got one should contact the *Chronicle*.

Billy couldn't believe his eyes. Billy's mum couldn't believe her eyes. But Billy's dad was grinning. 'Good, eh?' he said.

Billy's mum rounded on him angrily. 'What do you mean, good? What's good about it? Our Billy plastered all over the front pages! Good? You must be out of your mind. You're as bad as he is. You must both be mad.'

She turned on Billy. 'Why didn't you tell us about this?' she demanded. Then before he could answer she turned on his dad again. 'Did you know anything about this, Brian?'

Billy's dad shook his head. 'Yes, why didn't you tell us about this, Billy?' he asked gently. Billy had been wondering about that himself. He had thought about telling his mum and dad the evening before but somehow he hadn't got round to it. It had all seemed so unreal at home, almost as if he had dreamt it, that he had been afraid they would think he was making it up. He certainly would have told them if he had known it was all going to be on the front page of the *Chronicle*.

'Well, come on,' said his mum angrily. 'Answer your dad. Why didn't you tell us?'

But before Billy could speak there was a loud knocking on the front door.

'Oh blast,' said Billy's mum getting up to answer it. 'Don't you think I've forgotten about you,' she said, wagging her finger at Billy as she went towards the door. 'I want an answer.'

When she threw open the door she found two men, one with an expensive-looking camera hanging from a strap around his neck.

'Hello, love,' said one of the men. 'Billy Budge live here, does he?'

'Yes,' said Billy's mum angrily. 'What do you want? I'm his mum.'

'His mum?' said the man, grinning. 'No, you're having me on. You must be his big sister. You don't look old enough to be his mum.'

Billy's mum blushed. 'Well, I have been told I look young for my age,' she said, forgetting all about being angry.

'We're from the *Gazette*, love,' said the

man. 'We just want to have a word with the young genius, and of course his proud parents. Jim, we must get some pictures of this lovely lady.'

'Oh, no,' said Billy's mum, 'I haven't done my hair yet today.' And she rushed off to get tidied up for the photographer.

5

Billy Becomes a Star

Two important things happened to Billy in the week following the *Daily Chronicle* story — school broke up, and he became a star.

The end of the summer term leading up to the long holiday was always an exciting time for Billy as he looked forward to getting away from school and to all the fun he would have with his friends in the holidays. But it had never been like this before.

As soon as his mum had got over the shock of seeing Billy's name in the *Chronicle* she became as pleased and proud as his dad and decided to take time off from her job to be with him in the holidays. She had talked excitedly to the man from the *Gazette* and told him she had always known Billy was going to be

73

successful one day because a gypsy woman had told her so when he was a baby. The *Gazette* man had taken all this down in his notebook while the photographer took pictures. One of them appeared on the front page of the paper the next day with a caption underneath which read: 'Proud parents Brian and Pauline Budge with their child prodigy son, Billy.'

When Billy's mum read it she called upstairs to his dad, shaving in the bathroom: 'Brian, what's a child prodigy?'

'It means he's clever,' came the answer.

'I already knew that,' she said, giving Billy a hug.

It was not only the *Gazette* that called. Local and national newspapers and radio and television stations all rang wanting more information, more pictures, more details of what Billy was like as a young child, what his friends were like, what he did in his spare time, did he have any brothers or sisters, how long his parents had been married, where they met, why and how and when and a thousand other things.

And it wasn't only Billy and his mum

and dad who seemed to be asked questions from morning to night. The other reporters got more interviews with Miss Penny and with Mr Fletcher who by this time had become such a hero in the newspapers for trying to help Billy find the answer he wanted that his boss had quite forgotten about firing him and was thinking of giving him a better job.

But it was mainly Billy who interested the newspapers, thanks to the *Chronicle* story, and the competition that soon started.

When sums began flooding into the *Chronicle* office the editor had called for his reporter again. 'Good man,' he told him, 'you did an excellent job on this story, but it isn't going to stop there. This thing is really taking off. It's capturing the imagination of the public and if we handle it right we can double our daily sales. We are going to turn this into a competition and we are going to give a £10,000 prize to the winner, the sender of the hardest sum.

'Think of it, Grant! This is summer, the time when newspapers have to start scratching around for news. The silly

season, when newspaper sales always go down. But we are not going to watch our sales going down. We are going to increase them in a way that will have our competitors green with envy. This little lad is going to make our fortune for us. The £10,000 prize will be nothing compared to what we will make in extra sales. Go and write a piece for tomorrow announcing that the *Chronicle* is sparing no expense to help this lad in his search for knowledge.'

When the competition was announced the whole thing really did catch on. Newspapers and television stations around the world used Billy's picture and told the story of his search for the hardest sum. People in Europe, America, Japan, in the Australian outback and in the jungles of Brazil came to recognize Billy's face, they read his story and began following with growing interest the daily bulletins issued by the *Chronicle* on what sums had been received, who had sent them, and which seemed the most likely winners.

Schoolboys, teachers, distinguished professors and learned lecturers flooded the *Chronicle* with sums and as the number of entries grew by the hundreds every day it began to look as if judging the competition would become a quite impossible job. But the editor had been right — there was a massive increase in sales and extra printing staff had to be taken on to run the press for twenty-four hours a day to try to meet the demand.

For Billy's family, life had become one long series of interviews and the phone seemed to ring non-stop with calls from reporters. Had Billy seen the latest sums in the *Chronicle*, they asked. Would he become a maths professor when he grew up? Was it true he could do logarithms at the age of two? (Billy scratched his head and wondered what logarithms were.) Was his dad a computer expert? ('That would kill them down at the garage,' said Billy's dad and he laughed loud enough for the neighbours to hear.) Would Billy be judging the competition for the hardest sum? ('You must be joking,' his mum replied.)

Even in the middle of the night the Budge family was not left in peace. Newspapers from the far side of the globe, where our night is their day, rang to get the latest information on the *Chronicle* competition and ask yet more questions. Billy's mum would grope for the phone in the early hours of the morning and find herself talking to a reporter in Sydney or New York or Rio de Janeiro.

At first the publicity was great fun. People Billy hardly knew would stop him in the street as he went to the paper shop for the *Chronicle* and tell him what a clever lad he was. Other ladies would stop Billy's mum in the supermarket and say: 'Hello, dear. I saw you on television. You're the lady what her little boy has got that competition in the newspaper, aren't you?'

Neighbours they hardly knew suddenly greeted them like long-lost friends. 'You looked marvellous on TV last night,' they would say. Or, 'I saw your picture in the paper again this morning.' The Budges suddenly seemed to have made hundreds of new friends and every time they went out they made even more.

Sackfuls of letters arrived for Billy by every post from all over the country and the world. There were letters from school-boys who thought Billy must be very clever at maths and asked him for help with their homework. There were letters from people who loved doing sums and others from people who thought sums were boring and should be done away with. The competition seemed to give people the chance to say things they had been thinking ever since they were doing sums at school. Everyone seemed to have something to say about the competition and most of them seemed to think that they were the only ones who were right. Billy looked at them all and scratched his head, wondering if his mum would make him answer them all the way she did when his Aunt May wrote to him on his birthday. 'We've got enough here already to paper the lounge,' his mum would say as the postman arrived with even more letters.

'You'll be able to paper the kitchen as well, now,' the postman would say with a grin.

Almost every day a TV crew from a British television station or from a station abroad knocked on the door wanting to talk to Billy and his mum and dad. Before that Billy had not often watched the news on television and had never given any thought to how it was actually gathered, and if someone had asked him to describe the average television crew he wouldn't have had a clue. But he quickly learned that each crew included a cameraman, a sound recordist and a reporter, and some crews had extra people to help the cameraman or the sound man. The other thing that all the crews had in common

was masses of gear, including massive
spotlights, cameras, recording machines
and what seemed like miles of cable, all of
which they would set up in the living room
while Billy's mum dashed about telling
them to mind they didn't scratch the
furniture, fetching them cups of tea and

rushing round with a cloth in case they spilt any on the carpet.

Another thing that Billy had never realized was that many foreign television stations had their own crews in Britain to report on any news here that people back home in their own countries might be interested in. One day it was a Japanese TV crew which came to the door, with four smartly dressed little men who smiled and bowed very politely. 'Bow back,' Billy's mum hissed at him. So Billy bowed back and the Japanese men bowed back until it looked as if they were all going to be stuck there bowing on the doorstep until Billy's dad came home. On another day it was an American crew with drawling men who, much to Billy's surprise, called him 'sir', and his mum 'ma'am'. Other crews came from French, Italian, Australian and Middle Eastern TV stations and even from some countries in South America.

Some of the interviews they taped were shown on the news or on magazine programmes in Britain but most of the crews sent their tapes straight overseas to their own countries. 'All this trouble and we won't even get to see ourselves on television,' Billy's mum would say to the foreign TV men as she threaded her way across the obstacle course of cables and bits of equipment set up yet again in the living room. But Billy was fascinated by it all and after the TV men had patiently answered his questions about the equipment they would often let him work the cameras or recording machines.

But as the days went by everyone in the Budge household began to get very fed up with it all. Billy's mum became more and more irritable and when his dad came home from work she would say angrily: 'It's all right for you. You're not here all day long. I'm fed up with it. I can't get any peace, what with the phone ringing and reporters knocking on the door all day. I can't get out to the supermarket or even the corner shop without having people pointing me out and asking me all about Billy. I can't find time to do anything except answer the phone, go to the door and answer stupid questions all day long. I'm fed up with it.' Billy's dad would nod his head sympathetically and put his arm round her comfortingly. No one blamed Billy for it all but he knew that he had started it and not being told off or blamed just made him feel worse, especially when he saw his mum get so upset.

To Billy, the best thing of all was that his gran, who had seen him in the papers and on television, rang up from his Aunt May's. 'What's my clever little man been up to then?' she said. 'Gran saw you on the TV last night and I thought. "That's my little man there on television," and Gran was ever so proud of you.' Billy smiled. If it made his gran proud of him it was worthwhile, after all.

What Billy disliked most was not going out to have fun with his friends as he usually did in the holidays. Weeks went by and it seemed as if he would be back at school for the start of the autumn term without ever going out or seeing any of his pals.

But one morning when he answered a knock at the door expecting to find another reporter looking for an interview, he was surprised and pleased to see Jumbo Gibbs standing on the doorstep.

'You coming out?' asked Jumbo.

'Yeah,' said Billy eagerly, then as an

afterthought, 'I'd better just ask my mum. She's in the bath.' He shouted up the stairs: 'Mum, can I go out with Jumbo?'

'You know you can't,' came the angry reply. 'I've only just finished getting you tidied up for those *Chronicle* people who are coming this morning. I'm not having you going out and getting filthy. Don't you dare go out now, Billy!'

'Awwwww, Mum,' said Billy pleadingly.

'No, Billy, and that's final. Why don't you take Jumbo up to your room to play.'

'Want to go upstairs and play?' Billy asked reluctantly.

'Yeah, all right,' said Jumbo.

They sat on Billy's bed and tried to think of something they could do without going out or getting dirty.

'You seen anyone from school?' asked Billy.

'Yeah, I saw Croaker and some of the others yesterday,' said Jumbo. 'They'd all seen you on TV and in the papers.'

'Yeah,' said Billy. It seemed like ages since he had seen the other members of class 14b.

'What's it like?' asked Jumbo.

'What's what like?'

'Being on TV?'

Billy thought about what it was like. 'It's all right,' he said. Then after a pause he added: 'It's not as good as you think it's going to be.'

'I wouldn't mind being on TV,' said Jumbo.

'My mum says she gets a headache as soon as she sees another TV crew on the doorstep,' said Billy.

'Why?'

'Because they mess up the living room with their equipment and it all takes ages.'

'It doesn't take ages on TV,' said Jumbo. 'It only takes a minute or two to answer some questions.'

'But it isn't really like that,' said Billy.

'Why not?'

'Dunno. I suppose nothing is ever as simple as you think it's going to be,' said Billy wistfully.

After a while Jumbo said: 'Doesn't your mum like you being on TV then?'

'Dunno,' said Billy. 'She did at first. But she got fed up with it.'

'I wouldn't get fed up with it,' said Jumbo, imagining himself surrounded by reporters asking him questions while photographers took his picture. 'It'd be just like being a film star.'

'Perhaps film stars don't have as much fun as you think they do,' said Billy. 'Anyway, perhaps their mums don't get pestered by reporters.'

'Do you wish you hadn't done it then?'

'Done what?'

'Asked Miss Penny that question,' said Jumbo.

Did he wish that, Billy wondered. Perhaps if he'd known all the trouble it would cause for his mum and dad. But then again. . .

Billy's thoughts were suddenly interrupted by his mum's voice from downstairs. 'Billy!' she shouted. 'Come on! They're here.'

6
The Winner

Every day during the holiday the *Chronicle* reporter, Craig Grant, had visited Billy's home or telephoned to get more information for the stories that the newspaper had published daily along with the latest news on the competition. After the first stories, news of the competition was taken off the front page and put on an inside page, but there was always a note on the front page telling people where to turn for the search for the hardest sum and it became the first thing that many readers looked at every morning.

Craig Grant had racked his brains every day for new things to say about Billy and the competition to keep people interested in the story. He had interviewed just about all of Billy's relatives, including some he hadn't seen for years, about how proud they were and what a bright baby he had been.

There were interviews with the teachers from Billy's old infant and junior schools, interviews with neighbours, with the man from the paper shop where Billy went to fetch the *Chronicle*, and with the little old lady down the road who walked her dog in the mornings and always said 'Hello' to Billy as he passed her on his way to school. Other stories included interviews with famous mathematicians, with people who had sent sums in to the *Chronicle*, and people who claimed to have mystical powers and said they could predict the result of the competition. (The mystics all turned out to be wrong, but no one remembered that and the *Chronicle* certainly wasn't going to remind them.)

After weeks of desperately thinking up new ideas for stories Craig Grant was very glad that the competition was almost over. He felt as if he would rather be thrown out of his office window than be made to write yet another story about Billy and his question. If it wasn't for frequent chats with the editor, Grant might not have been able to go on as long as he had. 'You are doing an excellent job,' the editor would say to him when Grant had been summoned up to his grand office on the top floor of the newspaper building. 'Our sales are at record levels thanks to you and this lad Billy Whatshisname. The other papers are green with envy. This has been the best thing ever to happen to our circulation. Keep it up, Grant. Keep it up. What are you going to give us on the competition in tomorrow's paper?'

'I don't know, sir,' Grant would say. 'I'm totally out of ideas. I just can't think of another thing to do on the competition. I really think it's time someone else took over for a while. . .'

'Nonsense,' the editor would say, interrupting him. 'I have complete faith in you, Grant. I know you'll give us something good tomorrow. Keep it up, Grant. Keep it up.'

And so Grant would slump back into his swivel chair in his tiny office and rack his brains for yet another story about Billy, or his family or the competition or something.

But now all that was over. Grant had come to make the final arrangements for the announcement of the winner and the presentation of the £10,000 prize the next day, at which Billy and his mum would, of course, be guests of honour.

Billy and Jumbo found Grant waiting in the living room with a photographer and a smartly-dressed young lady. Billy's mum was just telling them how excited she was about the ceremony.

'Hello, Billy,' said Grant. 'Who's this?' he asked, pointing at Jumbo. Billy introduced them. 'Great,' said the reporter. 'Get some pictures, Bert.'

The camera shutter clicked and Billy and Jumbo blinked, dazzled by the blinding flashes of light.

'Well, tomorrow's the day,' said Grant. 'Are you excited, Billy?'

'Yes,' said Billy, trying hard to feel that he was and wondering, at the same time, why it was that he didn't seem to feel at all excited.

'Would you say you were really over-whelmed with excitement?' asked Grant.

'I suppose so,' said Billy, wondering how it felt to be overwhelmed with excite-ment. How did you tell when you were? Mr Grant must know, thought Billy. He must have seen lots of people over-whelmed with excitement.

'Billy,' said Grant, 'I want you to meet our promotions manager, Miss Veronica Lively.' He motioned towards the smartly-dressed young lady who peered at Billy through large tinted glasses.

'My goodness,' she said, smiling broadly, 'so this is the little maths expert.'

Billy looked around, thinking she must be talking to someone else, but she was definitely looking at him and she suddenly grabbed his hand and shook it warmly.

'It's a very great pleasure,' said Miss Lively, beaming at Billy.

'Veronica will be in charge of all the arrangements for the presentation tomorrow,' said Grant.

'Isn't it exciting, Billy,' said his mum. 'Tomorrow's the day!'

'Yes,' said Billy, trying hard to grin, and not succeeding very well.

Later, as Billy and Jumbo sat on the settee munching peanut butter sand-wiches that his mum had made for them before she went out to the shops, Billy mused: 'At least tomorrow I should get the answer I wanted, I suppose.'

'You don't sound very happy about it,' Jumbo observed between mouthfuls of sandwich.

Billy had to agree that it was true and it had been worrying him. 'It is exciting . . .' he began, 'but. . .'

'But what?'

'I just didn't expect anything like this.'

'What did you expect?' asked Jumbo, looking puzzled.

'I don't know,' said Billy. 'It just seems an awful lot of trouble to go to. I just thought Miss Penny could tell me the answer and that would be all there was to it.'

'That isn't what you told the reporter.'

'No,' said Billy. 'I couldn't say something like that after all the trouble he went to.'

'Suppose not,' said Jumbo, munching the last of his sandwich. 'Do you think it's all been a waste of time, then?'

Billy thought hard about it and he just couldn't believe that it had been. Not after all the trouble so many people had gone to and the problems it had caused for

Miss Penny, Mr Fletcher and his mum and dad. 'It makes you think,' he said eventually.

'About what?'

'Not about anything special,' said Billy, struggling to find words for what he wanted to say. 'It just makes you think about things. When you learn about things you didn't know anything about, it makes you think about other things and wonder why they are how they are.'

Jumbo blinked at his friend. 'Oh,' he said, wondering what on earth Billy was going on about.

They sat in silence for a while, as Jumbo puzzled about what Billy meant. Finally Billy said: 'Jumbo?'

'Yeah?'

'What's your name, I mean your real name?'

Jumbo looked even more puzzled. 'Why do you want to know?'

'I don't know,' said Billy. 'I just wondered.'

After a long pause Jumbo said: 'It's David.'

'David,' said Billy as if he had never heard the name before. 'So why does everybody call you Jumbo?'

'Dunno,' said his friend. 'They just do.'

'Can I call you David?' asked Billy.

'Yeah, all right,' said his friend.

'You two look very serious,' said Billy's mum as she dashed in from the shops with some things for tea. 'What are you talking about?'

'Just some things,' said Billy.

'Early night, tonight, Billy,' his mum shouted through from the kitchen as she banged about with the pots and pans preparing a meal. 'We've got an early start in the morning.'

The next morning she scrambled out of bed as soon as the alarm went off, shouting shrilly: 'Brian! Billy! Come on, get up. We'll miss that train. Come *on*!'

Billy gingerly uncovered an ear and heard the sound of running bathwater from down the corridor and his mum calling again for him to get up. Reluctantly he pulled back the bedclothes and crawled out of bed.

Coming out of their bedrooms at the same time and both still half asleep, Billy and his dad bumped into each other. His dad gave him a grin and ruffled his hair.

'It's the great day today, eh, son?' he said.

'Yes, Dad. I wish you were coming with us.'

'So do I,' said Billy's dad, 'but I just can't take the time off from work right now. Your mum will look after you. She's certainly excited about it. I haven't seen her so excited about anything for ages.'

'Is she overwhelmed with excitement?' asked Billy curiously.

'Eh? Oh, you mean like the newspapers say?'

'Yes, that's it,' said Billy.

'I don't know,' said his dad, scratching his head. 'Yes, I suppose you could say she is.'

'How do you tell?' asked Billy.

'She shouts a lot,' said his dad.

'Are you two ever going to get moving,' screamed a shrill, muffled voice from the bathroom. 'If we miss that train I shan't go. I'm not going to turn up there late. We've only got an hour left to get ready *and* get to the station.'

'See what I mean?' said Billy's dad with a grin.

Despite his mum's fears they were ready in time and even had a few minutes to spare. As Billy's dad said, his mum was more excited than she had been about anything for ages and she had put on her best cream-coloured skirt and jacket with a pretty frilly blouse, her best high heeled shoes and her reddest lipstick and she wafted clouds of perfume everywhere she went.

Billy had on the grey suit he had been bought for his sister Helen's wedding. His mum had bought him a new shirt and tie which Billy thought must have been made especially to strangle people slowly. He wriggled and squirmed inside the collar and felt very uncomfortable. 'Do keep still, Billy,' his mum kept saying.

'Have a good day, son,' said Billy's dad. 'I wish I could be there, but I'll be thinking of you. I'm really proud of you.' He hugged Billy and it looked almost as if there might be tears glistening in his eyes. Suddenly there was a loud honking noise in the street outside and Billy's mum shouted: 'It's the taxi!'

As they hurried out into the street, wafting perfume and 'goodbyes' they were greeted by loud cheers and saw to their surprise that the street was packed

with people. Billy blinked in astonishment and looked around at the cheering crowd. All their neighbours were there and many of the people they knew in the area. Billy looked around and saw the man from the newspaper shop and the lady who said 'Hello' to him as she walked her dog.

'Well done, Billy,' they all shouted. 'Good luck.' And the man from the newspaper shop led them all in three rousing cheers. Billy waved to everyone and felt like a hero. In fact he was something of a hero to the people in the street because Billy and his question had made the street famous. Reporters and television crews had come there and interviewed and photographed many of the neighbours until they felt as if they were celebrities, and it was all because of Billy. Now they felt it was just as much their day as Billy's and they cheered and waved and waved and cheered until the taxi taking Billy and his mum to the station had completely disappeared out of sight.

A large, black limousine was waiting at the station in London and it quickly whisked them away through the busy streets. Billy stared wide-eyed at the tall, imposing buildings and the mass of people and traffic thronging the streets. At last the car drew up outside a very grand-looking hotel. Hung across the front of the building was a huge banner which read:

'The *Daily Chronicle* Reveals the Hardest Sum in the World Here Today.'

Waiting on the steps were the *Daily Chronicle* reporter, Craig Grant, and Veronica, the smartly-dressed young lady who was in charge of all the arrangements. Veronica rushed forward and shook them each warmly by the hand. 'Mrs Budge. Billy,' she beamed at them. 'It's a great pleasure.' She led them into a massive lobby, as big as a cathedral, where people were rushing around in all directions. Hotel staff in smart crisp uniforms were hurrying backwards and forwards to the hotel conference hall where the ceremony was to be held, with food for the buffet lunch. There were carefully-arranged plates of cold meat, bowls of cool green salad, delicious-looking sauces, baskets of bread, mouthwatering cakes, savoury rolls and delicious desserts. Others were carrying cutlery, plates, glasses, cups, tablecloths and flowers and plants to decorate the room and the tables.

Smart young women, dressed like Veronica in blue suits with their names on small labels on their lapels, were hurrying around with clipboards looking very official and comparing their notes with one another. Billy thought he had never seen so many people rushing so much, not even in the corridors at school when the bell had just gone, and he began to feel some of the excitement that everyone else seemed to be feeling.

Veronica looked hurriedly at her watch. 'We're almost ready,' she said, trying hard to beam. 'We're just making a few last-minute preparations.' And she whisked Billy and his mum away to a quiet lounge for coffee.

When she collected them again half an hour later it was as if a miracle had happened. The lobby was magically clear except for a few hotel guests reading newspapers and when Veronica led them into the conference hall everything was exactly in place as if it had always been just where it was. All the crockery and cutlery, plates, bowls and baskets of food and all the plants and flowers were carefully and colourfully laid out on the shining white tablecloths on tables around the room. The hall was full of people, who were being handed drinks by white-coated waiters balancing trays on one hand. Some were guests or staff of the *Daily Chronicle*, who stood around noisily chatting as they sipped their drinks. Others were competitors who had sent in likely winning entries and it was easy to tell them from the others because they stood on their own, looking nervous and uncomfortable as the suspense mounted.

Billy and his mum were ushered to the place of honour on the top table at the far end of the room. It looked very grand, mounted on a small dais and surrounded by many plants that it was like sitting in a jungle clearing. Billy peered nervously over the top of the plants at the huge hall and squirmed inside his stiff collar. 'Do keep still, Billy,' his mum hissed. 'Sit up straight.'

There was a sudden flash of colour from the far end of the room as red-uniformed trumpeters formed up on either side of the entrance. Veronica appeared in the doorway and at a signal from her the trumpeters launched into an ear-splitting fanfare. As the last notes died away a dinner-jacketed man nearby called out loudly. 'My lords, ladies and gentlemen, please welcome your host, the editor of the *Daily Chronicle*.'

Everyone stood up and clapped loudly as the editor entered, waving and smiling to acknowledge the applause. He strode down the length of the hall to the top table and turned to smile and wave again. Then he turned to Billy, grabbed his hand and shook it as if intent on pulling Billy's arm off. 'So this is young . . . young . . . the young man who started it all,' beamed the editor, thinking of all the extra newspapers they had sold. 'And you must be his mum. A clever little boy you've got there. We certainly won't forget his name in a hurry.'

The editor took the centre of the table and began a long speech about how the competition had come about and what a prodigy Billy was. Billy blushed and tried to hide behind the plants and the people who had sent in competition entries wriggled about on their chairs and wished the editor would just get on with it and announce the winner. When the speech was finally over the editor beckoned to a man waiting beside a large machine at the side of the hall.

'And now,' said the editor, 'I'll call for the winning entry flashed directly to our telex machine here from the university where distinguished mathematicians have fed all the entries into the computer for analysis and selection.'

Billy couldn't help smiling to himself as he remembered that it was the university computer that had got the *Chronicle* involved and really started everything off. He wondered if it would call the editor 'ape face'.

The man in charge of the telex machine hurried over and whispered something nervously in the editor's ear. 'What?' said the editor angrily and he muttered fiercely to the man who hurried back to the machine and began urgently tapping out messages on a keyboard.

The editor turned to the audience and tried hard to beam at them as if nothing was wrong. 'But first, ladies and gentlemen,' he said. 'I would like to say a few words about the measures we are taking to maintain the remarkable increase in sales that we have lately experienced.'

The people who had sent in sums

groaned and slumped in their chairs as the editor launched into what seemed likely to be another very long speech. But suddenly he was interrupted by the telex machine which sprang into life, printing noisily onto a long roll of paper. For a moment there was silence in the hall except for the chattering of the machine, then someone shouted excitedly: 'It's coming through.' There was a sudden scramble for the telex machine and people elbowed each other for places where they could see the message being printed out. Line after line of figures were quickly imprinted onto the paper roll. An old gentleman with large, thick glasses and long side whiskers recognized the figures and began dancing round excitedly calling out: 'I've won, I've won.'

Finally the machine fell silent and the man who was in charge of it tore off the long roll of printed paper. The girls in blue suits began ushering people back to their seats and finally, with some difficulty, got them all sitting down, even the old man who had kept rushing round excitedly telling everyone that he was the winner.

The editor looked at the sum, now torn up into half a dozen separate sheets, and frowned as if it was Chinese. With the help of Veronica and Craig Grant he finally found a name and address on the top sheet and announced the winner, who was indeed the old gentleman. He leapt up and danced around calling: 'I told you I'd won. I told you.' There was a barrage of flashguns glaring and people cheered and clapped as the editor waved the sheets above his head and cried: 'This, ladies and gentlemen, is the hardest sum in the world.'

The editor was handed a sheet of details about the winner which he read out and then, as more camera flashes flared and everyone applauded, the old gentleman was presented with the £10,000 prize cheque. Afterwards he made a speech thanking the *Chronicle* for his prize and saying he had spent the whole of his life studying maths and now planned to take a long holiday in foreign parts thanks to the £10,000.

After much more applause the audience broke up and headed for the food, chattering excitedly amongst themselves about the result of the competition. Billy hung back behind his mum and as soon as he could he sneaked back to where he had been sitting. The hardest sum in the world lay discarded and forgotten on the table. Billy picked it up and began trying to make sense of it. He was scratching his head over a particularly difficult page of figures when Craig Grant and the elderly gentleman came along.

'So what do you think, Billy?' asked the reporter with a grin.

'I can't quite understand it,' said Billy slowly. 'It's a difficult sum, isn't it?'

The old gentleman leaned over and glanced at the sheet Billy was holding. 'That's the answer,' he said. 'The sum is on those other sheets.'

'Oh,' said Billy, even more puzzled. 'It's rather hard, isn't it?'

'It's the hardest sum in the world,' said the old gentleman proudly. 'That's official.'

'Great, eh?' said the reporter.

Billy just looked at it and scratched his head.

7

Another Journey

Between Billy's house and the park was the busy High Street and a number of quiet streets with big, old houses that all ran down in the direction of the park. Billy was walking back along one of these streets kicking aimlessly at a drink can that had been thrown down on the pavement.

He was thinking again about the final of the *Daily Chronicle* competition. It had been exactly two weeks before, but to Billy it seemed like two years because his life was so different since. On the evening of the prizegiving there had been a few calls from newspapers and television stations and the *Chronicle* and other papers had carried the story next day of the end of the search for the world's hardest sum. But then the publicity stopped as sud-

denly as it had begun. The constant interruptions of reporters and photographers knocking on the door demanding interviews and pictures ceased as the newsmen moved on to new stories elsewhere. The phone that had rung constantly day and night suddenly went dead. Billy and his family and the search for the hardest sum were yesterday's news in old newspapers that people used as packing or wrapped round fish and chips.

For Billy and his mum and dad the silence was eerie. His mum would wake up in the middle of the night wondering why the phone wasn't ringing with calls from America, Australia, Thailand, Hong Kong and all the other places where people had eagerly followed the story. The phone calls and demands for interviews had become a daily nuisance that they had all learned to put up with and when those things were no longer there they found themselves longing for just one more phone call, just one more knock on the door, but none came.

The neighbours who had stood in the street and cheered Billy and his mum on their way to the competition final had gone back to their usual day-to-day routine and the Budge family had tried to go back to theirs. The saga of the hardest sum was a story that the neighbours would sometimes remember and tell their friends and relatives or strangers that they met in the doctor's waiting room or in a railway carriage, but it was no longer a part of their daily lives. It was all in the past.

Despite Billy's pleas, his mum had gone back to work after the competition was over. 'I've already had this year's holiday and next year's,' she had told him. 'If I don't go back to work now I won't have a job to go back to.' So she had gone off, leaving Billy to try to find something to fill the rest of the holiday. Every lunch-time she popped in for twenty minutes to see that he was all right and was having something to eat. The rest of the time Billy mostly sat around watching television. He didn't feel like fishing or playing football or doing any of the other things with his friends that he usually did in the holidays. He didn't even feel like seeing any of the others from class 14b. He was sure they would ask him what it was like to be a celebrity and be interviewed on TV and had the competition been exciting and what was the hardest sum in the world like. He didn't want to talk about it. He didn't even want to think about it.

Billy gave the drink can a final, determined kick and it went careering off the pavement into the gutter. He watched it come to a stop on a drain grating, then he trudged on slowly towards home. He had only gone out that afternoon because Jumbo had called for him, but it hadn't been any fun. They had hung around in the park for a while but there didn't seem anything that Billy wanted to do or talk about and when he saw some of the others from his class he made an excuse that he had to be home early. As he trudged along with his socks dropping down to their lowest possible point Billy shook his head sadly at the way his holiday had gone. It had seemed to start so well only to end like this and there was now only one more day to go before he went back to school, back to Miss Penny's maths class.

His mum was already home when he got in and when she saw how sad he looked she hadn't the heart to tell him off about his dirty shoes or drooping socks. She just said: 'Tea won't be long, love.' Billy nodded and tried to smile.

When his dad arrived home he found Billy in the living room staring at the television set. 'Hello, son,' he said. 'What's on television?'

'Nothing much,' said Billy absent-mindedly.

His dad gave him a worried look and sat down beside him. 'So what have you been doing with yourself?' he asked.

'Nothing much.'

'Nothing much? When I was a lad you couldn't keep me in during the holidays. I was always out somewhere playing with my friends and having fun. I was off first thing in the morning and they didn't see me at home again until it was dark.'

Billy said nothing. He seemed to be wrapped up in his own thoughts.

'Are you all right, son?' his dad asked gently.

'Yes, I'm fine, dad.'

'We haven't heard much from you since the competition ended. You've never

116

really told me anything much about it, you know.'

'Sorry, Dad, I meant to, but. . .'

'What is it that's bothering you, son? Can't you tell me?'

'It's just that . . . I didn't understand it.'

'Understand what?' asked his dad. 'The sum they printed in the paper? I'm not surprised. I couldn't understand it either. I shouldn't think anyone could. You could hardly read it for a start, it was in such small print.' His dad laughed but Billy still looked worried and serious. 'What did you expect?' his dad asked gently.

'I don't know,' said Billy shaking his head. 'Something else. I didn't think it would be like that. I thought I would be able to understand it . . . perhaps after they explained it to me.'

'But, Billy, it's the hardest sum in the world, son. You and I can't expect to understand it.'

'Why not?'

'Because we're no good at sums.'

'But what are they for if no one understands them?' asked Billy.

'Some people understand them, I suppose,' said his dad. 'People in colleges and universities. They understand them. They're the ones who make them up so they must understand them.'

'But if people make them up they must be for something, mustn't they?' asked Billy.

'I suppose they must be,' said his dad.

'I thought they could tell me what it was for,' said Billy, 'and then I would understand why it was important. I mean, it's no good if it doesn't do anything, is it, Dad?'

Billy's dad shook his head and wished he could say something that would help Billy stop feeling so sad. But Billy was already lost deep in his own thoughts again. He was trying, as he had tried so many times since the competition, to remember what he had really hoped to find out when he first asked Miss Penny his question, but that all seemed so far away now and all he had learned was that the hardest sum in the world was just one more sum he didn't understand.

A call of 'Tea's up' from the kitchen finally brought the conversation to an end just as another, also about the competition, was about to start at the offices of the *Daily Chronicle*.

One of the phones on the editor's large desk rang and when he picked it up he found himself speaking to another editor thousands of miles away.

'Hello,' said the caller, 'do I have the great honour of speaking to the British *Daily Chronicle* editor?'

'You have for the next thirty seconds,' snapped the editor. 'I'm about to go home.'

'Then I will be brief,' said the voice on

119

the crackling long-distance line. 'This is Mr Bannerjee, editor of the *Calcutta Daily Record* and your sums are rubbish.'

'What?' exploded the editor. 'What did you say?'

'Rubbish is what I am saying,' said Mr Bannerjee. 'That is what your sums are. Rubbish, rubbish, rubbish.'

'Now look here,' said the editor sternly, 'don't you talk to me like that.' He paused for thought and then added: 'What on earth are you talking about anyway?'

'It was your newspaper, was it not, that published the story of Billy Budge and the hardest sum in the world?'

'Billy who? Oh, yes, the little lad, Whatshisname. We did run something like that at one time. What about it?'

'I am telling you your sum is rubbish,' said the Indian.

'No, it isn't. It's the hardest sum in the world.'

'No, it is not.'

'Yes, it is,' snapped the editor.

'No, it is not.'

'You can do better, I suppose?' said the editor sarcastically.

'Not I personally, you understand,' said Mr Bannerjee. 'But my newspaper has uncovered a challenger who says his sum can make yours look very jolly sick.'

'Does he? Well, saying is one thing, doing is something else entirely. If I believed everything everyone said they could do I wouldn't be where I am today. Now as I said I am about to go home. . . .'

'You mean you are not going to take up the challenge?' asked Mr Bannerjee angrily.

'If your man is so clever,' said the editor, 'he should have entered our competition. As far as I am concerned the whole thing was over and done with weeks ago and I do not propose to start it up again.'

'I see,' said Mr Bannerjee. 'Well, in that case I shall just have to offer our story to another of your British newspapers. I am sure they would be only too pleased to be able to discredit the result of the competition that you caused so much fuss about.'

'I don't think they will be interested,' said the editor loftily.

'I am sure they will be,' said Mr Bannerjee.

So am I, thought the editor. It's just the sort of underhand thing they would do. It's certainly the sort of underhand thing I would do if I was them. 'On the other hand,' he said, 'we set out to leave no stone unturned in our bid to help that little lad . . . umm. . .'

'Billy Budge?' asked Mr Bannerjee helpfully.

'Yes, that's him,' said the editor. 'We pledged our help in his search for knowledge and we won't be found wanting whatever the cost or the difficulty. Get your man to give us a ring and we'll take details of his sum over the phone.'

'I am afraid that will not be possible,'

said Mr Bannerjee.

'All right,' said the editor, 'I'll tell you what, he can reverse the charges. Provided it's a fairly short sum.'

'No, no, you misunderstand me,' said Mr Bannerjee. 'He cannot be contacted by telephone.'

'He's not on the phone?' said the editor in astonishment. 'I thought everyone was on the phone these days.'

'I regret there are no phones where he lives.'

'No phones?'

'No. No phones. You must understand that this man is a mystic who has lived for many, many years in a cave in the foothills of the Himalayas.'

'How are we supposed to get in touch with him them?' asked the editor.

'There is only one way,' said Mr Bannerjee. 'You must send young Billy to meet him.'

'What? Are you mad? Do you know what that would cost?'

'I am reading in your newspaper that you would spare no expense to help young Billy in his search for knowledge,' said Mr Bannerjee.

'Well, yes,' said the editor defensively, 'but I didn't expect it to cost that much.'

'I am sure you will consider it money well spent if you can help young Billy.'

Hmmm, thought the editor, sales have been dropping off since the competition ended. Maybe this is just what we need to revive them. 'I'll do it,' he said.

Moments later he was getting through to his reporter. 'Grant,' he snapped, 'get me the parents of young Whatshisname who started off that competition about the sum.'

Billy and his mum and dad had just finished tea when the phone rang. His mum answered it and a look of surprise began to spread across her face. 'But . . . how can he possibly . . .' she said, trying hard to get a word in. 'He's got to go to school. . . Well, I can't take any more time off . . . oh . . . I see . . . yes, well . . . goodbye.'

'What is it, love?' Billy's dad asked as she put down the phone.

'That was the editor of the *Daily Chronicle*,' said Billy's mum. 'It looks as if Billy is going on another trip. That reporter is going to call for him tomorrow morning.'

'Where am I going?' asked Billy eagerly. 'To London again?'

'No, love,' said his mum. 'A bit further than that this time.'

8

The Hardest Sum of All

The next day *Chronicle* reporter Craig Grant called for Billy in a big limousine like the one that had met him at the station in London. But this time the car would take them all the way to London Airport.

'Do you know where we're going, Billy?' asked the reporter, smiling. Billy shook his head. 'We're going to the foothills of the Himalayas. What do you think about that, eh?'

'Will we be back by tomorrow?' Billy asked.

The reporter laughed. 'Tomorrow? No way. It's thousands of miles.'

Billy grinned and he looked out of the window and chatted excitedly. He had never been away from home before, except to the seaside and on trips to Aunt

May's and his sister Helen's house with his mum and dad. To be going away to the far side of the world on his own was such a great adventure that he hardly even minded the suit and shirt and tie his mum had made him put on.

'I'm not having you going about the world looking like a tramp,' she had said the night before. 'And make sure you put on some clean underwear. You might have an accident and have to go to hospital. What would the doctors and nurses think if you had dirty underwear on?' Then she had hugged him and said: 'You look after yourself and make sure you don't have any accidents.'

'Good luck, son,' his dad had said ruffling his hair. 'I hope you find what you're looking for.'

The big car whisked them quickly to the airport terminal for long haul flights and the reporter bought Billy sweets and comics in an airport shop as they waited for their plane.

When they got on board the massive aeroplane Billy thought it was the most exciting thing he had ever done. He had only to sit down and it would take him

away to the far side of the world. 'It's like a magic carpet,' said Billy, though to tell the truth it was really more like a huge bus with rows and rows of seats.

Stewardesses, smartly dressed in dark uniforms, went quietly up and down the gangway smiling and asking people to fasten their seat belts. After take-off they offered passengers tea and coffee, drinks and meals, snacks and more drinks until Billy thought he would burst if he ate or drank anything else.

It was a long journey and gradually drowsiness overcame Billy's excitement and he fell asleep. He woke with a start with the reporter shaking him and saying excitedly: 'Billy! Billy! We're almost there.'

As the plane coasted to a stop on the runway at Calcutta Billy noticed it was getting very much warmer and when they left the plane a solid wall of heat hit them.

'Billy, we'll have to get that collar and tie off you before you suffocate,' said the reporter loosening his own tie as sweat began dripping off his chin. Billy grinned. There were lots of good things about foreign travel, he thought.

A taxi was waiting outside the airport building to take them into the bustling city of Calcutta. The taxi honked and pushed its way through the crowds past street markets and bazaars to the offices of the *Record* where Mr Bannerjee welcomed them. He was a small, dark man in a spotless white suit who smiled constantly.

'Have you had a good journey?' he asked. 'You must be very tired. And I am sure you must be wanting a cold drink.' They both nodded eagerly.

As they sipped their drinks Mr Bannerjee said: 'Now perhaps you would like to know something of the man you have come to see.'

Their eyes widened with anticipation.

'He is an aged mystic,' said Mr Bannerjee, 'who has lived for many years — no one knows how many — in a cave in the lower foothills of the Himalayan mountains.'

'Is that in Tibet?' Billy asked.

'Not far from the Tibetan border,' answered Mr Bannerjee.

'Who is he?' asked the reporter. 'And what does he do?'

'He is called,' said Mr Bannerjee reverently, 'the Swami of Wami.'

'The what?' asked the reporter, laughing.

Mr Bannerjee ignored the interruption. 'He is a very famous holy man who spends

131

his life meditating. He is known throughout India as the wise one whose sayings are revered. We sent a messenger to him with a copy of your British *Chronicle* and he says the sum in it is rubbish. He says only he knows the secret of the hardest sum.'

'Well if I can get to talk to him perhaps we can all find out what it is,' said the reporter.

'I do not think that will be so,' said Mr Bannerjee.

'Don't you think he'll tell me?' asked the reporter.

'He will not see you,' said Mr Bannerjee.

'What? Are you kidding? Do you think my editor would spend all this money on sending me out here to see some old guy who won't even give me an interview? He'll go crazy when he hears this.'

'I am sorry,' said Mr Bannerjee, 'but the Swami is adamant. He will only see the young one.'

'You mean Billy?'

'That is correct.'

'Well, at least that's something, I suppose,' the reporter said doubtfully.

Mr Bannerjee smiled sympathetically. 'You have a long way to go,' he said. 'I will send one of my reporters with you as a guide because where you are going the people speak no English. Tonight you will stay in a very fine hotel in Calcutta. Tomorrow you start your journey.'

When they arrived at the railway station the next morning they found a crowd of Indian reporters and correspondents for papers in Britain, Europe, America and many other countries. People who had followed the search for the hardest sum had not yet forgotten Billy and most of the correspondents had been woken early by excited phone calls from their papers about this new quest. The news of Billy's journey had been broken by the *Daily Chronicle* that morning with a story and a picture of Billy boarding the plane to India. The reporters had quickly learned which train Billy was catching and were determined to stick to him no matter where he went.

Billy smiled to himself. It was nice to be a celebrity again though he was glad it would only be for a short time.

When their train drew in it was quickly

packed with hundreds of people and the ancient steam engine had to huff and puff very hard to get moving again. The journey was at first uncomfortably hot and sticky as they sped through the Indian countryside but as they went further north the weather became colder and colder and they were glad of the thick, warm clothing Mr Bannerjee had provided for them.

At last they had to leave the train and travel in an aged bus over rough, bumpy roads for many miles until, towards evening, they reached their destination, a small village at the foot of steep mountain slopes.

The Indian reporter who was acting as their guide pointed up the slope. 'Up there is the Swami's cave,' he told them.

'Up there,' gasped Billy, looking up to the summit of the range of mountains, capped in snow and almost hidden in the clouds.

'Oh, no, no, no,' laughed the reporter. 'You misunderstand me. The cave is only a short way up the mountain. We will go there in the morning.'

As Billy settled down to sleep that

night he wondered what he would learn tomorrow. Would the Swami really have the secret he hoped to find? What *did* he hope to find anyway? And how would the

Swami be able to tell him anything if he spoke only Indian and Billy spoke only English? Billy shrugged and closed his eyes. He was sure if it really was the secret he would know it. And he knew the Swami would find some way to tell him about it.

The next morning Billy and Craig Grant started up the steep slope towards the Swami's cave with the Indian reporter guiding them and the large group of correspondents, more used to sitting in their offices than climbing mountain slopes, puffing and sweating along behind. After almost two hours of hard climbing the Indian reporter stopped them and he and Billy went on alone to the mouth of the cave about two hundred metres away. While Billy waited the Indian went inside. He came out a few minutes later.

'The Swami is meditating,' he told Billy. 'We must wait.'

'How long for?' asked Billy.

'I do not know,' said the Indian. 'Sometimes he meditates for days. Or weeks. Or even for months.'

They waited hunched-up on the windblown slope for what seemed to Billy like ages, until suddenly they heard the sound of tapping on the rock inside the cave.

'Quickly,' said the Indian, 'he is ready, you must go in now.'

Billy hurried towards the mouth of the cave, excitement making his tummy tingle. He slipped inside and blinked as sweet-smelling smoke stung his eyes. As he gradually became accustomed to the dim light and the smoke he saw that he was in a large cavern, larger than he had expected. There was a small open fire burning low at the far end of the cavern and by straining his eyes Billy made out a dark figure sitting cross-legged beside it. The figure raised its head and Billy saw that it was an old man with a long beard, wearing a robe like a monk's habit. He raised a bony finger and beckoned Billy, motioning him to sit near. Billy sat down near the fire and crossed his legs. Despite the cold outside, the cave was pleasantly warmed by the glowing fire.

Billy waited a long time for the old man to speak and finally asked: 'Are you the Swami?'

The old man nodded his head gravely.

Billy was in awe of the serious-looking old man, but he screwed up his courage and asked: 'Please, sir, can you tell me. . .'

The old man held up a bony hand to silence him, then he motioned towards the fire. Billy stared at it but could see nothing except the crackling flames. They both sat for many minutes gazing into the flames. After a while Billy fancied he could see figures and faces. As the flames leapt and curled they made the shapes of countries, strange animals, exotic buildings, mountain ranges and all sorts of marvellous things. He wondered if that was what the old man had intended him to see. Then suddenly the Swami raised his head.

'Now, lad,' he said in a thick Northern accent, 'what d'ye want to know?'

Billy almost fell over backwards with surprise to hear a British voice and his eyes widened until they looked like two small blue saucers.

'Come on, come on,' said the Swami impatiently. 'I've a lot of meditating to do, d'ye know.'

But Billy could only stare open-mouthed with amazement.

'Cat got ye tongue?' asked the Swami.
The hard lines of his stern face relaxed
and his eyes twinkled. 'I reckon you were
expectin' somethin' different.'

139

'Yes,' gasped Billy. 'I thought you would be . . . well. . .'

The old man roared with laughter. 'It isn't only Chinamen and Indians as can do this, d'ye know. I were a miner in Yorkshire afore I come here, so long ago I can't remember. I figured if I were going to spend me life underground I might as well do summat worthwhile while I were there. The name's Billy, is it?' Billy nodded. The old man looked at him shrewdly. 'You'll ha' come about that sum,' he said.

'Yes, sir,' said Billy.

'Aye,' said the Swami, nodding. 'I'm none surprised. They know nothing, these professors, for all their computers and fancy talk. They dun't even teach you right at school.'

Billy stared in amazement.

'Tell me, lad, what one and one meks.'

'It's . . . it's . . . two, sir,' stammered Billy.

The old man snorted with laughter then gave Billy a shrewd stare. 'Is that all the' can teach you? That's a poor education and no mistake.' He suddenly uncrossed his legs and leapt up so nimbly that it took Billy completely by surprise. The old man beckoned with his long, bony fingers for Billy to follow and they made their way to the back of the cave. The old man drew aside a curtain covering an alcove to reveal a large cage of split bamboo full of mice hurrying and scurrying. There were dozens of them, all pure white with pink eyes, scrambling over one another and dashing up and down the sides of the cage.

'These are my little friends,' said the old man. 'They keep me company on long winter nights.'

'They're lovely,' said Billy, wide-eyed.

'Aye,' said the old man. 'D'ye know know how many I had to start with?'

Billy shook his head.

'I had one male and one female,' grinned the old man. 'Now you count 'em and tell me how many one and one meks. Go on, count 'em.' He snorted with laughter as Billy tried in vain to count the fast-moving little creatures. 'One and one meks two, eh?' snorted the old man in disgust. 'Human race started with just two people, so we're told. And how many of us are there now? Millions! It's the

141

same when you tek away. I'll bet the'
taught you one from two leaves one?'

Billy nodded.

'I'll tell you a story, lad,' said the old
man. 'I had two other mice afore. One of
'em died and t'other just pined away from
loneliness. So one from two left none.'

Billy tried hard to understand what the
old man had been saying but his thoughts
had been thrown into confusion.

The old man gave him a kindly smile.
'Dun't go bothering your head about it,
lad. It'll come to you in time.'

Billy wished he was so sure. 'But,
sir ...' he began, 'aren't sums mostly
about things, and not about people or
mice?'

'Things?' said the old man fiercely.
'Things? Look around you, lad, and tell
me how many things you see here.' He
gestured with his bony hand around the
large, bare cave. 'Do I have things? I do
not! And I'll tell you this for nowt, I'm a
sight happier sin' I came to this place
than I ever were when I lived where you
live and had *things*. The whole world's
mad on *things*. Folk must always have
this thing and that thing. They spend
their lives collecting things they've no

earthly use for and then die and leave 'em behind to other folk. Dun't you go that way, lad. I'll tell you this, the *things* a man needs he can carry in his pocket.'

The old man's face relaxed again into a kindly smile and he took Billy by the hand and led him down a rock corridor leading off the cave. They came to a crevice where the rock was split and Billy gasped as he found himself staring up at a breathtaking view of the Himalayas stretching as far away into the distance as he could see.

'Aye,' smiled the old man, nodding in agreement. 'It's beautiful. These are the things that matter, lad. Not the things they sell in fancy shops but the things created and set down here long 'fore you and I were ever thought of. D'ye know who set 'em here?'

Billy shook his head.

'No more do I,' said the old man, his eyes twinkling. 'But it might come to me sometime when I'm meditating.' He turned and gazed long and hard at the mountain range. 'Where's their arithmetic now then?' he asked. 'D'ye think you can say, tek one mountain range away from the world and it leaves so many? Think now, suppose some great hand could come out of the sky and pluck up this whole range of peaks stretching thousands of miles. Think of all the live creatures that live here as would be lost, aye, including me. Think of the beauty, the majesty and mystery of these peaks as would be lost for good, and all the little settlements at the foot of these mountains as would lose their shelter. Think of all these as would be lost to the world and would you tell me that all as would be lost is one *thing*?' The old man snorted in disgust at the idea.

Billy shivered as he began to feel the cold wind cutting through his warm clothes. The old man noticed and led him back to the fire where they sat cross-legged staring into the flames for some time. Billy tried hard to gather his scattered thoughts. He could understand now why the old man spent so much time meditating. There was so much more to think about than he had ever realized. Finally he began slowly: 'But . . . if all that is true . . . I mean . . . well . . . what is one and one?'

The old man smiled broadly. 'Anything,' he said. 'Or nothing.'

'Then ... what,' said Billy hesitantly, trying hard to understand how that could be and what it meant, 'I mean ... how do you know which it is?'

'You don't,' said the old man, still smiling at Billy's confusion.

'Then ... why do people ... I mean, why do they say you do know?'

'Now you have it, lad,' said the Swami excitedly, as if he had been waiting patiently for Billy to reach this point. 'Now you have it! There's a lot that folk don't know, but it scares 'em not knowing so they make up the things they don't know. They make up sums and think they understand and control the things around 'em because they can count 'em up. They think all they have to do to understand the world is to make up ideas about what it's like and the world will oblige them by being like they claim it is. D'ye understand, lad?'

'I think so, sir,' said Billy, though he was not at all sure that he did.

'Aye, well think on, lad. Think on. It'll all come to you in time.' He eyed Billy shrewdly. 'Well, then,' he said, 'you'll think on't if you will. There's no more I can do for you.' He bowed his head and stared into the fire as he had when Billy first saw him. Billy hesitated, confused by all that had happened, and after a while the Swami lifted his head and looked at him.

'Are you still here, lad? What d'ye want now?' His face was stern but his eyes twinkled.

'Please, sir...' Billy hesitated. 'I was hoping ... well, I thought perhaps you could tell me ... what's the hardest sum in the world?'

'Dun't ye know that yet?' asked the old man with mock surprise. 'Maybe you aren't as clever as I took you for, after all. Look now, lad, follow this. Stand up. Now sit down. Raise your arms. Now lower 'em.' Billy looked in astonishment at the old man but obeyed his instructions. He was ever more astonished at the old man's next words. 'Can you move? Can you keep still?' Billy nodded. 'How? Why?' Billy gaped open-mouthed at the old man. 'How? Why?' the Swami repeated. 'How can you move your arms and legs, your

146

head and body, all independently? How is it you can keep your arms and legs still? Why don't they move all the time? Where did you get these powers? How did you get 'em? And why? Why are you able to move about at all? Plants can't. They live and breathe, just like you. They are born and die, they eat and drink, just like you. But they can't wave their stems or raise and lower their leaves and petals at will. Why can you an' they can't?'

Billy shook his head. 'I'd never even thought about it,' he said.

'Can you laugh?' asked the old man. 'Can you cry?' Billy nodded. 'Other creatures can move like you,' the old man said. 'The bear, the cat, the dog. Some monkeys can even chatter to sound almost like people. But which of 'em can laugh or cry? How can you do that and not them? And which creature has the power that you have to think and speak, to tell others of what you think and hear what they think? Why do you have that power when other creatures don't? D'ye know, lad?'

Billy, lost in amazement at all the things the old man had told him, could only shake his head.

'Ye dun't know much then,' grinned the old man. 'But no more do I. Nor does anyone. Holy men have studied for centuries without answering one o' them questions, without ever really *knowing* how or why any of it 'appened. You'll grow up into a man and do all sorts of things every day that might seem ordinary and usual but are really marvellous and magical because no one will ever do 'em just exactly the way you'll do 'em and because no one can ever explain why you're here and why you are the way you are and can do the things you do. Now do you understand?'

Billy's head was full of thoughts jumbling and tumbling over each other like the mice in the cage. He was lost and struggling in a sea of ideas. 'No, sir,' he said shaking his head sadly. 'I don't understand.'

'Why bless me, boy, *you're* the hardest sum in the world. You and me and everyone. All of us.' He saw the confusion in Billy's face and went on: 'You're the sum of a thousand abilities and gifts that no one can properly understand or explain.

148

No one knows why you have those gifts and abilities or why other creatures don't have them. We only know that you *do* have them. The sum of all those things is what makes you you and no other creature who ever lived and *that's* the hardest sum of all because no one will ever explain it or understand it.'

Billy nodded his head slowly. He was sure that it was as the Swami had said — it would come to him in time. But he thought he had begun to understand what the old man had been trying to tell him and making a start was all that mattered. As the old man had also said, there was a lot of meditating to do.

9
The Secret

The large crowd of pressmen were still sitting hunched-up against the cold on the hillside where Billy had left them.

When he came out of the cave and down the slope towards them they jumped up as fast as their cold, stiff limbs could carry them and crowded round him. Flashguns flared, reporters grabbed for their pens and notebooks with frozen fingers and others shoved microphones at him. They shouted at him: 'What did he say, Billy? What's the answer? Tell us what the secret is, Billy.'

Billy grinned at them. 'I can't tell you the secret,' he said.

There were cries of surprise and astonishment, then they shouted: 'What do you mean, you can't tell us? Why not?'

'If I told you the secret, it wouldn't be a

secret anymore, would it?' Billy replied.

'Oh, come on,' shouted the reporters. 'We've been waiting here for two hours in the freezing cold. Come on, just give us a clue. Just tell us a little bit of it, or the answer, or something.'

A reporter with a microphone pushed it at Billy and said: 'Just tell us the first few figures of the sum.'

'I can't,' said Billy.

'Sure you can,' said the pressman. 'Why not?'

'Because there aren't any figures in it,' said Billy.

'What kind of sum is that?' asked the man in astonishment.

'The hardest kind,' said Billy with a grin, and he strode off down the slope leaving the startled pressmen gaping at each other in amazement.

THE END

EATING ICE CREAM WITH
A WEREWOLF
by Phyllis Green

When Brad and Fat Nancy's parents go to Bermuda, they need a baby-sitter at short notice.

'Not Phoebe Hadley,' Brad pleaded. 'She almost drowned me once, and last time she baby-sat, I ended up in hospital. She always has a hobby she wants to try out on me. Please, anyone, but not Phoebe Hadley.'

But Mum and Dad were talking about Bermuda and Brad couldn't get a word in edgeways. All he could do was wait until Phoebe arrived . . .

Zany, outrageous Phoebe turned her stay into the most hilarious adventure Brad and Nancy had ever had; they never knew *what* was going to happen next! What could have caused the chicken to appear on Nancy's bed? Did they *really* eat ice cream with a werewolf?

0 552 524190

CORGI

TOM'S SAUSAGE LION
by Michael Morpurgo

It was Christmas Eve when Tom first saw the lion. His mother had sent him out to fetch logs – and there was the lion padding through the orchard with a string of sausages in its mouth! Tom couldn't believe his eyes and, worst still, when he rushed indoors to tell them, his family didn't believe him either.

There *was* a lion. Tom knew there was, knew that he hadn't dreamed it. So he sat up, night after night, waiting for the lion to return . . .

0 552 524182

Available soon from Corgi Books

MANY HAPPY RETURNS AND OTHER STORIES
by Kathryn Cave

Alice loathes all her birthday presents on sight
and finds a hilarious way of dealing with them
. . .

Cousin Roderick comes to stay and causes
chaos until a spider provides an unusual
solution . . .

The dreaded Mrs Bannerman terrorizes her
class when mystery messages from 'Billy
Molloy' appear on the blackboard. Who wrote
them?

And just what *are* James and Mary going to do
about the dinosaur in their garden?

These are just a few of the extremely funny and
perceptive stories in this new collection from
Kathryn Cave, author of the highly popular
Dragonrise.

0 552 524344

Available soon from Corgi Books

MYSTERY CAT
by Susan Saunders

Kelly Ann and Hilary soon discover that there
is something very special about the battle-
scarred grey tom they call Mystery Cat (M.C.
for short). He doesn't really belong to either of
them, he goes wherever he pleases – and the
local police know him well!

According to them, whenever there is a spot of
trouble, a crime or something fishy going on,
M.C. can usually be found on the scene. Kelly
Ann and Hilary find this hard to believe but,
sure enough, when someone in town starts
making counterfeit money, M.C. is in the thick
of it and the girls are soon caught up in a
thrilling, crime-busting adventure!

The first in a series of three about Mystery Cat
– the cat with nine lives and a sixth sense for
trouble!

0 552 524255

CORGI

EGBERT THE ELEPHANT
and other funny stories
by Barbara Ireson

'Who are you?' asked the mouse.
'I'm . . . I'm . . . I don't remember,' said Egbert.
'You don't remember,' said the mouse.
'I don't remember,' repeated Egbert.
'I don't remember much of anything.'

The hilarious way in which the mouse helps the little playroom elephant with his unusual problem gets this lighthearted collection off to a good start.

Other rib-tickling tales come from an array of well-known names including Norman Hunter, Beverly Cleary and Margaret Mahy.

0 552 524131

CORGI

If you would like to receive a Newsletter about our new Children's books, just fill in the coupon below with your name and address (or copy it onto a separate piece of paper if you don't want to spoil your book) and send it to:

The Children's Books Editor
Young Corgi Books
61–63 Uxbridge Road
Ealing
London W5 5SA

Please send me a Children's Newsletter:

Name: ....

Address: ....

....

....

All Children's Books are available at your bookshop or news-agent, or can be ordered from the following address:
Corgi/Bantam Books,
Cash Sales Department,
P.O. Box 11, Falmouth, Cornwall TR10 9EN

Please send a cheque or postal order (no currency) and allow 60p for postage and packing for the first book plus 25p for the second book and 15p for each additional book ordered up to a maximum charge of £1.90 in UK.

B.F.P.O. customers please allow 60p for the first book, 25p for the second book plus 15p per copy for the next 7 books, there-after 9p per book.

Overseas customers, including Eire, please allow £1.25 for postage and packing for the first book, 75p for the second book, and 28p for each subsequent title ordered.